SHAKESPEARE FOR EVERYONE

HAMLET

By Jennifer Mulherin   *Illustrations by* Roger Payne

CHERRYTREE BOOKS

Author's note

There is no substitute for seeing the plays of Shakespeare performed. Only then can you really understand why Shakespeare is our greatest dramatist and poet. This book simply gives you the background to the play and tells you about the story and characters. It will, I hope, encourage you to see the play.

A Cherrytree Book

Designed and produced by
A S Publishing

First published 1988
by Cherrytree Press Ltd
327 High Street
Slough
Berkshire SL1 1TX

Reprinted 1991, 1993, 1994, 1997
First softcover edition 1994
Reprinted 1995, 1997, 1998, 2001

Copyright this edition © Evans Brothers Ltd 2001

British Library Cataloguing in Publication Data
Mulherin, Jennifer
    Hamlet, (Shakespeare for everyone)
    1. Drama in English, Shakespeare, William.
    Hamlet - Critical studies - For schools
    I. Title II. Series
    822.3'3

ISBN 1 84234 033 6

Printed in Hong Kong through Colorcraft Ltd

Contents

Hamlet *and the Elizabethan court*

Hamlet is a play about kingship, loyalty and revenge. Most of the play takes place in the Danish court at Elsinore. Many of the young men in *Hamlet*, such as Laertes, Horatio, and Rosencrantz and Guildenstern were courtiers, as was Hamlet himself.

The finery in which Elizabethan courtiers dressed themselves is well illustrated in this portrait of Richard Sackville, 3rd Earl of Dorset. He was a patron of the playwright, Ben Jonson.

A nobleman's privilege

In Shakespeare's time, all the rulers of Europe had a court and a number of courtiers who served and attended upon the ruler at court – but not anyone could become a courtier. Only noble folk, who had a title, could attend court. Even the very wealthy were excluded, unless they were fortunate enough to be able to buy a title or were given one because of services to the country or the ruler.

In Queen Elizabeth's time, for example, many rich people were ennobled because they had given money to help fight the wars abroad – against, for instance, the Spanish Armada– or for the continuing troubles in Ireland.

The expenses of court life

Although a gentleman had to be well-born to be a courtier, he also had to be fairly rich since life at court was expensive. Not only was he expected to dress in fine clothes, he also had to take part in all kinds of exclusive sports and entertainments, and he had to keep horses, carriages and his own retinue of servants. Some nobles simply could not afford these expenses, so they only visited court from time to time; others were fortunate enough to be members of the king's or queen's household and received a salary, as well as having many of their day-to-day expenses paid.

The court on tour

Unlike many rulers in her time, Queen Elizabeth believed in keeping in touch with her subjects. Every summer she toured the country, staying at the large estates or palaces of

The procession of Queen Elizabeth to Blackfriars. Seated under a richly decorated canopy, she is carried by her courtiers and ministers and followed by elegantly dressed ladies of the court.

noble people. On these occasions, she took her entire household with her, so her host was obliged to house and entertain a great number of people – always, of course, in lavish style, as befitted the Queen. This was a very expensive business and a few days' visit could cost the country gentleman several thousand pounds.

The education of a courtier
In Elizabethan times, young noblemen were often sent abroad to be educated at a foreign university or to visit a foreign court. Hamlet, for example, returned from his studies in Germany on the death of his father and, at the beginning of the play, Laertes goes off to Paris to study. While abroad, the young men were expected to acquire several foreign languages. French and Spanish were the languages spoken at almost all the courts of Europe. They also learned about music, art and literature. Many young men visited Italy where the Italian Renaissance was flourishing. They admired the architecture in Florence and the paintings of Titian in Venice, and when they returned to England, they often commissioned paintings of themselves and built houses in the grand Italian style.

The courtier's behaviour
One of the most popular books in circulation at that time was a work by an Italian nobleman, Count Castiglioni, called *The Book of the Courtier*. It contained detailed advice about how a courtier should behave and what sort of man he should aim to be. This book had been reprinted many times and was popular throughout the whole of Europe. All young gentlemen followed the instructions laid down in this book.

Castiglioni insisted that a gentleman be courageous and skilled in the use of weapons. This meant that the young

Sir Philip Sidney, an Elizabethan poet and courtier. As a young man, he visited the courts of France, Austria and Italy. He wrote a series of sonnets called Astrophel and Stella *and a romance called* Arcadia, *which were much admired – and imitated – at the time. He was killed in battle at the age of 32. As he lay dying, he passed a cup of water to another dying man saying, 'Thy need is greater than mine.'*

nobleman learned fencing, so that if his or his family's honour were insulted, he could challenge his opponent to a duel – as Laertes does to Hamlet.

A sporting gentleman

The courtier had to be a skilled rider and especially good at hunting. Both Elizabeth I and James I were very keen hunters, so it was necessary for their courtiers to be good at this sport. Falconry was another popular out-of-doors sport, and so was swimming. Swimming was a favourite pastime with some of Elizabeth's courtiers; on one occasion, she was forced to ban a swimming race from Westminster to London Bridge organized by one of her noblemen.

The ritual of courtship and love

Above all, the courtier knew how to treat a lady politely and courteously. He was able to dance and make pleasant conversation. If he admired a lady, he wrote poems or stories, praising her beauty or her honour. Hamlet, for example, wrote 'words of . . . sweet breath' to Ophelia. To become betrothed to a lady, it was necessary to ask her father's permission to court her. Sometimes this was refused if the young man was not rich enough or not well connected. Not everyone married for love, and young girls were often forced into marriage with old but rich or powerful men.

One of the dangers of court life was that there were always intrigues, as well as entertainments. People fell in and out of favour very quickly if they did not know how to flatter the right people. Many a courtier was banished from court not because he was dishonourable or bad-mannered but because he had committed some slight offence which earned the disapproval of the Queen or one of her ministers.

Shakespeare's greatest play?

Many people believe that *Hamlet* is Shakespeare's greatest play. It is certainly one of the most popular and, for an actor, the opportunity to play the role of Hamlet is the mightiest challenge in his career.

This famous painting of Ophelia is by the 19th-century painter, Sir John Everett Millais.

A good mystery story

Hamlet contains some of the best-remembered lines in all Shakespeare's works, and it is also a powerful story of evil and revenge. Scholars have written a great deal about this play – pointing out how complicated a person Hamlet is – but, when it is acted on stage, it tells a gripping tale that is not at all difficult to follow. In this play more than many others, the characters are like living people. The audience follows their actions, thoughts and feelings and becomes involved with them. Was Hamlet really mad for a time, or was he only pretending? Did the Queen really love her son? Was Hamlet really in love with Ophelia? If he was, why did he treat her so cruelly? Hamlet is like a good mystery story, because people still ask these questions after seeing the play.

A revenge tragedy

Although this play is usually known as *Hamlet,* its full title is *The Tragical History of Hamlet, Prince of Denmark.* This told the Elizabethan audience straight away that the play was about the death of a noble hero. Revenge tragedies, in which the hero fights for justice and revenge before dying, were very common at this time. Usually they were full of violent action with lots of bloodthirsty details, which the Elizabethans loved. Thomas Kyd, who was writing plays just before Shakespeare, wrote a famous revenge tragedy called *The Spanish Tragedy,* which remained popular right through Shakespeare's lifetime.

Where Shakespeare found his story

Thomas Kyd probably wrote another play called *Ur-Hamlet* but the text has not survived. Scholars think, though, that it had much the same story as Shakespeare's *Hamlet.*

The story of Hamlet is also found in a Danish history book written by Saxo Grammaticus in the 12th and 13th centuries. This history was not translated into English until 1608, some years after Shakespeare wrote *Hamlet,* but it had been published in French. Shakespeare may have read the French version because many of the details of his story are the same. It tells the story of Amleth, whose mother is

The Spanish Tragedy:

Or,

Hieronimo is mad againe.

Containing the lamentable end of *Don Horatio,* and *Belimperia*; With the pitifull Death of Hieronimo.

Newly Corrected, Amended, and Enlarged with new Additions, as it hath of late beene divers times Acted.

LONDON

Printed by *Augustine Mathewes,* for *Francis Grove,* and are to bee fold at his Shoppe, neere the Sarazens Head, upon Snovv-hill. 1633.

The title page of the 1633 edition of The Spanish Tragedy *by Thomas Kyd. Although written more than 40 years before, this play was frequently performed and revised. Kyd died around 1594, about seven years before* Hamlet *was written.*

Woodcut of a petard, a small war machine. The common saying, 'hoist with his own petard' (which means, literally, to be blown up by your own bomb) comes from Hamlet.

called Gerutha; the names 'Hamlet' and 'Gertrude' are very similar to these.

Shakespeare never invented the stories of his plays but always took them from older tales. Whatever story he borrowed for *Hamlet*, the play was a great success and the Elizabethans loved it.

When Shakespeare wrote Hamlet

It is often difficult to say when Shakespeare wrote a play because they were not written down and published until some time after they had been performed. *Hamlet* was probably written in 1601 because in the play Shakespeare refers to a company of boy actors who had taken the theatres by storm just before then. Shakespeare often mentions current events in his plays and this has helped scholars to work out when he wrote them.

A foreign setting

Shakespeare set many of his plays in foreign lands, but it is unlikely that he ever travelled abroad himself. As with many of this other plays, Shakespeare makes no attempt to recreate a real Danish court, although he does use Danish names for two characters: Rosencrantz and Guildenstern. The court and courtiers are thoroughly English. Shakespeare's theatre company played at court on numerous occasions and he knew many courtiers. Shakespeare's friend and patron, the Earl of Southampton, was a well-known Elizabethan courtier and like many of them fell out of favour several times. He was, for example, imprisoned in the Tower of London, for supporting the Earl of Essex's rebellion in Ireland, although he was later released.

Shakespeare, the actor

We know that Shakespeare spent some part of his career in the theatre as an actor. One of the most famous speeches in *Hamlet* is the instructions to the actors on how to play their roles. He warns them to speak their lines 'trippingly on the tongue', without waving their hands about too much. He is particularly stern on clowns who play their parts for 'laughs'. He says, '. . . let those that play your clowns speak no more than is set down for them – for there be some of them that will themselves laugh, to set on some quantity of barren spectators to laugh too, though in the meantime some necessary question of the play be then to be considered. That's villainous, and shows a most pitiful ambition in the fool that uses it.' As a playwright and an actor, Shakespeare was very well aware of how a play should be presented on stage – and his advice to actors is just as important today as it was then.

A depiction of Hamlet with his father's Ghost on the battlements of Elsinore Castle. This illustration is by the 19th-century French artist, Eugene Delacroix, who produced a series of pictures of Hamlet.

The story of Hamlet

The guards of Elsinore Castle in Denmark have seen a Ghost on the battlements. It looks like the father of Prince Hamlet who died only two months before. They ask Horatio, a young nobleman and a friend of the Prince, to watch with them and to talk to the Ghost. When it appears, it does not speak, and disappears from sight.

The new King of Denmark

The new King of Denmark is Claudius, Hamlet's uncle who has just married the Prince's mother, Gertrude. He allows Laertes, the son of his Lord Chamberlain, Polonius, to return to Paris and urges Hamlet to cast off his mourning.

Hamlet is still distressed by his father's death and deeply upset that his mother has married barely two months afterwards. He longs for death and condemns his mother with the words, 'Frailty, thy name is woman.'

Hamlet's longing for death

O! that this too too solid flesh would melt,
Thaw and resolve itself into a dew ...
How weary, stale, flat, and unprofitable
Seem to me all the uses of this world.

Act I Sc ii

Polonius bids farewell to his son, advising him on how a young man should behave.

A ghostly meeting

Hamlet, meanwhile, has gone to the castle battlements with Horatio. When the Ghost appears, he speaks to Hamlet, as the spirit of his dead father. The Ghost tells how he was

> **Polonius's advice to his son**
> *Neither a borrower, nor a lender be;*
> *For loan oft loses both itself and friend,*
> *And borrowing dulls the edge of husbandry.*
> *This above all: to thine own self be true,*
> *And it must follow, as the night the day,*
> *Thou canst not then be false to any man.*
>
> Act I Sc iii

murdered by Claudius and asks Hamlet to revenge his death. Hamlet asks Horatio to keep the meeting secret saying, 'There are more things in heaven and earth, Horatio, Than are dreamt of in your philosophy.'

Hamlet feigns madness

Hamlet decides to find proof of his uncle's wickedness. He is determined to kill the King, and pretends to be mad in order to trick him. Ophelia, Laertes' sister, who has been courted by Hamlet, notices his strange behaviour. She tells her father, Polonius, who decides that Hamlet is lovesick for Ophelia.

Claudius, the King, is also worried about Hamlet's behaviour. He sends for Rosencrantz and Guildenstern, old school friends of Hamlet, and asks if they can find out what is wrong with him.

Hamlet soon discovers that they are messengers from the King. He describes his melancholy to them.

Hamlet's plot to trick the King

Hamlet learns that a group of travelling players are to perform at Elsinore Castle. Hamlet asks the actors if they will add a scene to their play – it resembles the way in which his father was murdered. If Claudius reacts to the scene on

16

Hamlet's melancholy

I have of late, – but wherefore I know not, – lost all my mirth, forgone all custom of exercises; and indeed it goes so heavily with my disposition that this goodly frame, the earth, seems to me a sterile promontory; this most excellent canopy, the air, look you, this brave o'erhanging firmament, this majestical roof fretted with golden fire, why, it appears no other thing to me but a foul and pestilent congregation of vapours. What a piece of work is a man! How noble in reason! how infinite in faculty! in form, in moving, how express and admirable! in action how like an angel! in apprehension how like a god! the beauty of the world! the paragon of animals! And yet, to me, what is this quintessence of dust?

Act II Sc ii

stage, Hamlet will know that the King is guilty. He says to himself, '. . . The play's the thing, Wherein I'll catch the conscience of the king.'

Hamlet spurns Ophelia

The King and Queen decide to see if Hamlet is suffering from lovesickness. They arrange for Ophelia to be alone with Hamlet, but where the King and Polonius can eavesdrop on the conversation. Hamlet ponders on death and asks whether it is better to live or die.

Hamlet on life and death

To be, or not to be: that is the question:
Whether 'tis nobler in the mind to suffer
The slings and arrows of outrageous fortune,
Or to take arms against a sea of troubles,
And by opposing end them? To die: to sleep;
No more; and, by a sleep to say we end
The heart-ache and the thousand natural shocks
That flesh is heir to, 'tis a consummation
Devoutly to be wish'd. To die, to sleep;
To sleep: perchance to dream: ay, there's the rub;
For in that sleep of death what dreams may come
When we have shuffled off this mortal coil,
Must give us pause. There's the respect
That makes calamity of so long life;

Act III Sc i

Hamlet spurns Ophelia's love with cruel words, and she cries out in despair at the change in him.

Hamlet rejects Ophelia

. . . Get thee to a nunnery, go; farewell. Or, if thou wilt needs marry, marry a fool; for wise men know well enough what monsters you make of them. To a nunnery, go; and quickly too. Farewell.

Act III Sc i

The King now knows that it is not love that disturbs Hamlet. He suspects Hamlet of evil plans and decides to send him to England.

The play's the thing

Before the play takes place in front of the court, Hamlet advises the actors on how to play their parts.

Hamlet's instructions to the players

Suit the action to the word, the word to the action; with this special observance, that you o'erstep not the modesty of nature; for anything so overdone is from the purpose of playing, whose end, both at the first and now, was and is, to hold, as 'twere, the mirror up to nature; to show virtue her own feature, scorn her own image, and the very age and body of the time his form and pressure. Now, this overdone, or come tardy off, though it make the unskilful laugh, cannot but make the judicious grieve ... O! there be players that I have seen play, and heard others praise ... that I have thought some of nature's journeymen had made men and not made them well, they imitated humanity so abominably.

Act III Sc i

Hamlet carefully watches the reactions of Claudius and his mother to the play. 'The lady doth protest too much, methinks,' is Gertrude's response, but the King is disturbed. When the actors reach the point where the Player King is poisoned, Claudius stops the play. Frightened and guilty, he rushes from the hall. Hamlet is now convinced that Claudius murdered his father and he is determined on revenge.

20

A chance to kill the King

The King now realises that Hamlet knows of his murderous deed. Alone, Claudius tries to pray for forgiveness but finds it difficult. Hamlet, seeing him alone, rejects the chance to kill him. If the King's prayers were heard, argues Hamlet to himself, Claudius might be forgiven and would not suffer the fires of hell.

Polonius behind the arras

Hamlet has been summoned to see his mother and she agrees that Polonius should hide behind the arras, or tapestry curtain, to listen to their conversation. Hamlet speaks harshly to his mother, threatening her, and Polonius cries out, alarmed for her safety. Hamlet, believing it to be the King, draws his sword and thrusts it through the curtain. Polonius falls dead at his feet.

The Queen, convinced that her son is mad, tells the King of Polonius's death. Claudius knows that the blow was intended for him and insists that Hamlet leave for England at once.

Ophelia's madness

Soon after Hamlet sets out for England, it becomes obvious that Ophelia has gone mad because of her father's death and the loss of Hamlet's love. 'When sorrows come, they come not single spies, But in battalions,' observes Claudius.

Laertes, who has heard of his father's death, rushes back to Denmark. He is shocked by Ophelia's insanity. She strews flowers and sings, oblivious of her surroundings.

Claudius urges Laertes to revenge

Claudius convinces Laertes that Hamlet is responsible for Polonius's death and also for Ophelia's madness. When they learn from a messenger that Hamlet has not gone to England but is returning to court, they set up a plan to kill him.

Claudius advises Laertes to challenge Hamlet to a fencing match. Laertes agrees but says that he will add poison to the tip of the sword. To make sure that Hamlet dies, Claudius decides to add poison to the wine Hamlet will drink during the duel.

The death of Ophelia

When the Queen informs them that Ophelia has died by drowning, Laertes is even more intent on revenge.

Ophelia's death

There is a willow grows aslant a brook,
That shows his hoar leaves in the glassy stream;
There with fantastic garlands did she come,
Of crow-flowers, nettles, daisies, and long purples,
That liberal shepherds give a grosser name,
But our cold maids do dead men's fingers call them:
There, on the pendent boughs her coronet weeds
Clambering to hang, an envious sliver broke,
When down her weedy trophies and herself
Fell in the weeping brook. Her clothes spread wide,
And, mermaid-like, awhile they bore her up;
Which time she chanted snatches of old tunes,
As one incapable of her own distress,
Or like a creature native and indu'd
Unto that element; but long it could not be
Till that her garments, heavy with their drink,
Pull'd the poor wretch from her melodious lay
To muddy death.   Act IV Sc vii

At the graveyard

Hamlet on his return to Elsinore has been met by Horatio in the graveyard outside the city. Here the grave diggers are preparing a fresh grave. Hamlet talks to the grave diggers and learns that one of the skulls dug up is that of his father's court jester, Yorick. It reminds him of happier times.

Hamlet remembers Yorick

Alas! poor Yorick. I knew him, Horatio; a fellow of infinite jest, of most excellent fancy; he hath borne me on his back a thousand times; and now ... Where be your gibes now? your gambols? your songs? your flashes of merriment, that were wont to set the table on a roar? Not one now, to mock your own grinning?   Act V Sc i

Horatio and Hamlet discover that the grave is for Ophelia. Hamlet declares his love for Ophelia, but Laertes insists that the fencing match take place.

25

The fatal duel

The fencing match begins, but during it there is a scuffle and both Hamlet and Laertes are cut with the poisoned sword. The Queen picks up the wine meant for Hamlet, and before the King can stop her, she drinks it and she dies. Hamlet picks up the poisoned sword and kills the King.

Hamlet's death

Laertes dies and it is clear that Hamlet, too, is dying. Horatio wants to drink the poisoned wine in order to die with Hamlet, but Hamlet insists that he remain alive to tell Hamlet's story and clear his name.

Before he dies, Hamlet appoints the young Norwegian prince, Fortinbras, as his successor to the throne. As Hamlet dies in Horatio's arms, Horatio bids him a last farewell.

At that moment, Fortinbras arrives at the Danish court from Poland to find a scene of devastation. The play ends with a tribute to Hamlet by Fortinbras.

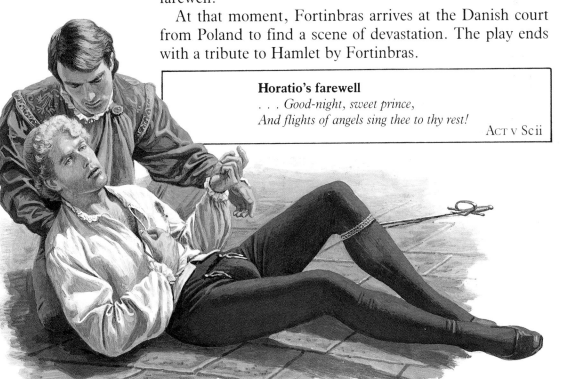

Horatio's farewell
. . . Good-night, sweet prince,
And flights of angels sing thee to thy rest!

Act v Sc ii

The play's characters

Hamlet

Ophelia on Hamlet's nature
O! What a noble mind is here o'erthrown:
The courtier's, soldier's, scholar's, eye, tongue, sword;
The expectancy and rose of the fair state,
The glass of fashion and the mould of form,
The observ'd of all observers . . .

Act III Sc i

Hamlet

Hamlet is one of the most complicated of all Shakespeare's characters. Sometimes he is gentle and thoughtful, but on numerous occasions throughout the play he is cruel and bitter – especially with his mother and Ophelia. Although we see him as a sensitive person who thinks deeply about the meaning of life, he is also a man of action. He plans and carries out his revenge quite ruthlessly, pretending he is mad in order to achieve his ends. Hamlet's behaviour is often odd and uncontrolled, and he even apologises to Laertes for being 'punished, With sore distraction', blaming his 'madness.' He seems to have violent swings of mood. He is brave in battle, honest and forthright. He is a loyal and honourable man who, according to Fortinbras, would have made a good ruler. He is an intriguing character. Was he really mad? Or was he only pretending? His cruelty to Ophelia and his unfeeling response to the death of Polonius can, perhaps, be excused if he was mad. Hamlet is not an easy person to understand, and many experts have tried to explain his contradictory behaviour. This is why he is one of the most interesting characters ever created by Shakespeare.

Polonius

Thou wretched, rash, intruding fool

Polonius is an old man but a responsible member of the King's household. He is the father of Laertes and Ophelia. He loves talking to anyone who is willing to listen to him, but Hamlet regards him as an old fool. Although he talks too much, as many old people do, some of his words are wise. His advice on how a gentleman should behave and dress is very sensible. He says, 'Costly thy habit as thy purse can buy, But not express'd in fancy: rich, not gaudy; For the apparel oft proclaims the man.'

Ophelia

Ophelia is beautiful, kind and gentle. She is an innocent girl and a dutiful and loving daughter, who is willing to follow her father's advice. When, however, she meets Hamlet there is no doubt that she loves him deeply. When Hamlet rejects her love, she cries out in despair at the change in him, pitying herself as well as him. Ophelia's madness is caused by Hamlet's rejection, and by the death of her father. She becomes a pathetic creature who wears flowers and sings songs about the loss of a loved one. She simply cannot endure the suffering that has befallen her.

Polonius

Ophelia

Ophelia's cry of despair
And I, of ladies most deject and wretched,
That suck'd the honey of his music vows,
. . . O! woe is me,
To have seen what I have seen, see what I see!
Act III Sc i

Claudius

Gertrude

Claudius

O! my offence is rank, it smells to heaven; It hath the primal eldest curse upon't; A brother's murder!

Claudius killed his brother because he wanted to be King, and to marry his brother's wife. He is an evil man who is prepared to murder Hamlet in order to keep his throne. But like most of Shakespeare's villains, he is not totally wicked; he does feel remorse and guilt for what he has done. He tries to pray for forgiveness but knows that it is useless. He feels sympathy for the mad Ophelia but his human qualities are outweighed by his evil ones. He is the person who is the cause of the play's tragedy.

Gertrude

Gertrude is not an evil woman but she is rather fickle. She grieves for only a short time after her husband's death, and her speedy remarriage upsets Hamlet very much. She seems to have destroyed his faith in the fidelity of women. She is easily led and rather selfish, but she shows affection for Ophelia, and love for her son – even if she does not understand him. 'The queen his mother, Lives almost by his looks', observes Claudius. Gertrude's dying words are a cry to her son.

The King's love for Gertrude

She's so conjunctive to my life and soul,
That, as the star moves not but in his sphere,
I could not but by her.

30

The life and plays of Shakespeare

Life of Shakespeare

1564 William Shakespeare born at Stratford-upon-Avon.

1582 Shakespeare marries Anne Hathaway, eight years his senior.

1583 Shakespeare's daughter, Susanna, is born.

1585 The twins, Hamnet and Judith, are born.

1587 Shakespeare goes to London.

1591-2 Shakespeare writes *The Comedy of Errors*. He is becoming well-known as an actor and writer.

1592 Theatres closed because of plague.

1593-4 Shakespeare writes *Titus Andronicus* and *The Taming of the Shrew*: he is member of the theatrical company, the Chamberlain's Men.

1594-5 Shakespeare writes *Romeo and Juliet*.

1595 Shakespeare writes *A Midsummer Night's Dream*.

1595-6 Shakespeare writes *Richard II*.

1596 Shakespeare's son, Hamnet, dies. He writes *King John* and *The Merchant of Venice*.

1597 Shakespeare buys New Place in Stratford.

1597-8 Shakespeare writes *Henry IV*.

1599 Shakespeare's theatre company opens the Globe Theatre.

1599-1600 Shakespeare writes *As You Like It*, *Henry V* and *Twelfth Night*.

1600-01 Shakespeare writes *Hamlet*.

1602-03 Shakespeare writes *All's Well That Ends Well*.

1603 Elizabeth I dies. James I becomes king. Theatres closed because of plague.

1603-04 Shakespeare writes *Othello*.

1605 Theatres closed because of plague.

1605-06 Shakespeare writes *Macbeth* and *King Lear*.

1606-07 Shakespeare writes *Antony and Cleopatra*.

1607 Susanna Shakespeare marries Dr John Hall. Theatres closed because of plague.

1608 Shakespeare's granddaughter, Elizabeth Hall, is born.

1609 *Sonnets* published. Theatres closed because of plague.

1610 Theatres closed because of plague. Shakespeare gives up his London lodgings and retires to Stratford.

1611-12 Shakespeare writes *The Tempest*.

1613 Globe Theatre burns to the ground during a performance of Henry VIII.

1616 Shakespeare dies on 23 April.

Shakespeare's plays

The Comedy of Errors
Love's Labour's Lost
Henry VI Part 2
Henry VI Part 3
Henry VI Part 1
Richard III
Titus Andronicus
The Taming of the Shrew
The Two Gentlemen of Verona
Romeo and Juliet
Richard II
A Midsummer Night's Dream
King John
The Merchant of Venice
Henry IV Part 1
Henry IV Part 2
Much Ado About Nothing
Henry V
Julius Caesar
As You Like It
Twelfth Night
Hamlet
The Merry Wives of Windsor
Troilus and Cressida
All's Well That Ends Well
Othello
Measure for Measure
King Lear
Macbeth
Antony and Cleopatra
Timon of Athens
Coriolanus
Pericles
Cymbeline
The Winter's Tale
The Tempest
Henry VIII

Index

Numerals in *italics* refer to picture captions.

Acknowledgements
The publishers would like to thank Morag
Gibson and Patrick Rudd for their help in
producing this book.

Picture credits
p.1 Governors of Royal Shakespeare
Theatre, p.3 Victoria & Albert Museum
(photo Bridgeman Art Library), p.5 Private
collection, p.7 National Portrait Gallery,
p.9 Tate Gallery (photo Bridgeman Art
Library), p.13 John B. Freeman & Co.